Gearhe

FORMULA 1 CARS

PETER BODENSTEINER

BLACK
RABBIT
BOOKS

BOLT

Bolt is published by Black Rabbit Books
P.O. Box 3263, Mankato, Minnesota, 56002.
www.blackrabbitbooks.com
Copyright © 2017 Black Rabbit Books

Design and Production by Brad Norr and
Michael Sellner
Photo Research by Rhonda Milbrett

Library of Congress Control Number: 2015954673

HC ISBN: 978-1-68072-029-7   PB ISBN: 978-1-68072-259-8

Printed in the United States at CG Book Printers,
North Mankato, Minnesota, 56003. PO #1790 4/16

Web addresses included in this book were working and appropriate
at the time of publication. The publisher is not responsible for broken
or changed links.

Image Credits
Corbis: Christopher Morris,
23 (car), 26–27; David Madison,
12–13; Reuters, 20–21, 32; Dreams-
time: Jordan Tan, 9 (engine); Markwaters,
29 (Senna); Patrickwang, 18–19; Getty: Mark
Thompson, 11; Rainer W. Schlegelmilch, 4–5;
SAEED KHAN/AFP, 15; iStock: Henrik5000, 9
(car); mevans, Back Cover, 1, 6–7; mik38, 3, 17;
Vlok, 24–25; Newscom: akg–images, 28 (race);
Shutterstock: Asmati Chibalashvili, 24–25, 31;
Ebic, 28 (moon); Ken Tannenbaum, 29 (towers);
PhotoStockImage, 23 (flag); RATOCA, 28–29 (car
design); ZRyzner, Cover
Every effort has been made to contact copyright holders for material reproduced in this
book. Any omissions will be rectified
in subsequent printings if notice is
given to the publisher.

CONTENTS

CHAPTER 1

LOUD and Fast

The Formula 1 (F1) car screams down the track. It's going almost 200 miles (322 kilometers) per hour. Suddenly, the driver slams on the brakes. Tears from his eyeballs hit the **visor**. He makes a quick turn and rockets away.

Don't Blink

In an F1 race, about 20 cars speed around
a track. The race starts with all the cars
sitting still. When the starting lights go out,
the cars speed away. At the end of the race,
drivers look for the checkered flag. The first
car to drive past the flag wins.

By the Numbers

F1 cars are the fastest race cars in the world. They turn easily and speed up quickly. They slow down even faster.

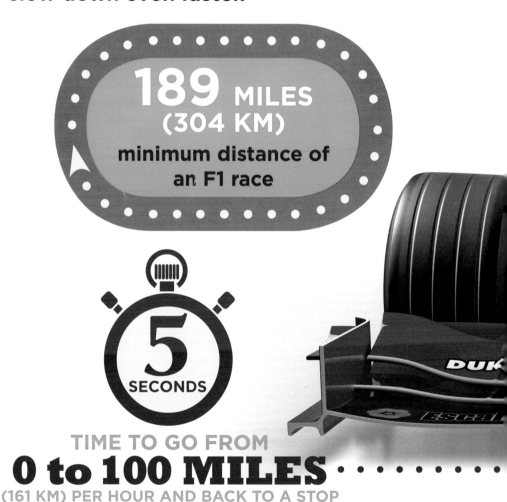

189 MILES
(304 KM)
minimum distance of an F1 race

5 SECONDS

TIME TO GO FROM
0 to 100 MILES ·········
(161 KM) PER HOUR AND BACK TO A STOP

750

HORSEPOWER OF AN F1 ENGINE

ABOUT
1,500 POUNDS
(680 kilograms)

WEIGHT OF AN F1 CAR

$300 MILLION

MONEY A TOP F1 TEAM SPENDS EACH YEAR

CHAPTER 2

A Global Sport

F1 races are held all around the world. Drivers earn points for each race. At the season's end, the driver with the most points is World Champion.

Before the 1970s, teams painted their cars in **national** colors. But companies soon saw that many people watch F1 races. Today, companies pay teams to paint **ads** on the cars. F1 cars are like moving **billboards**.

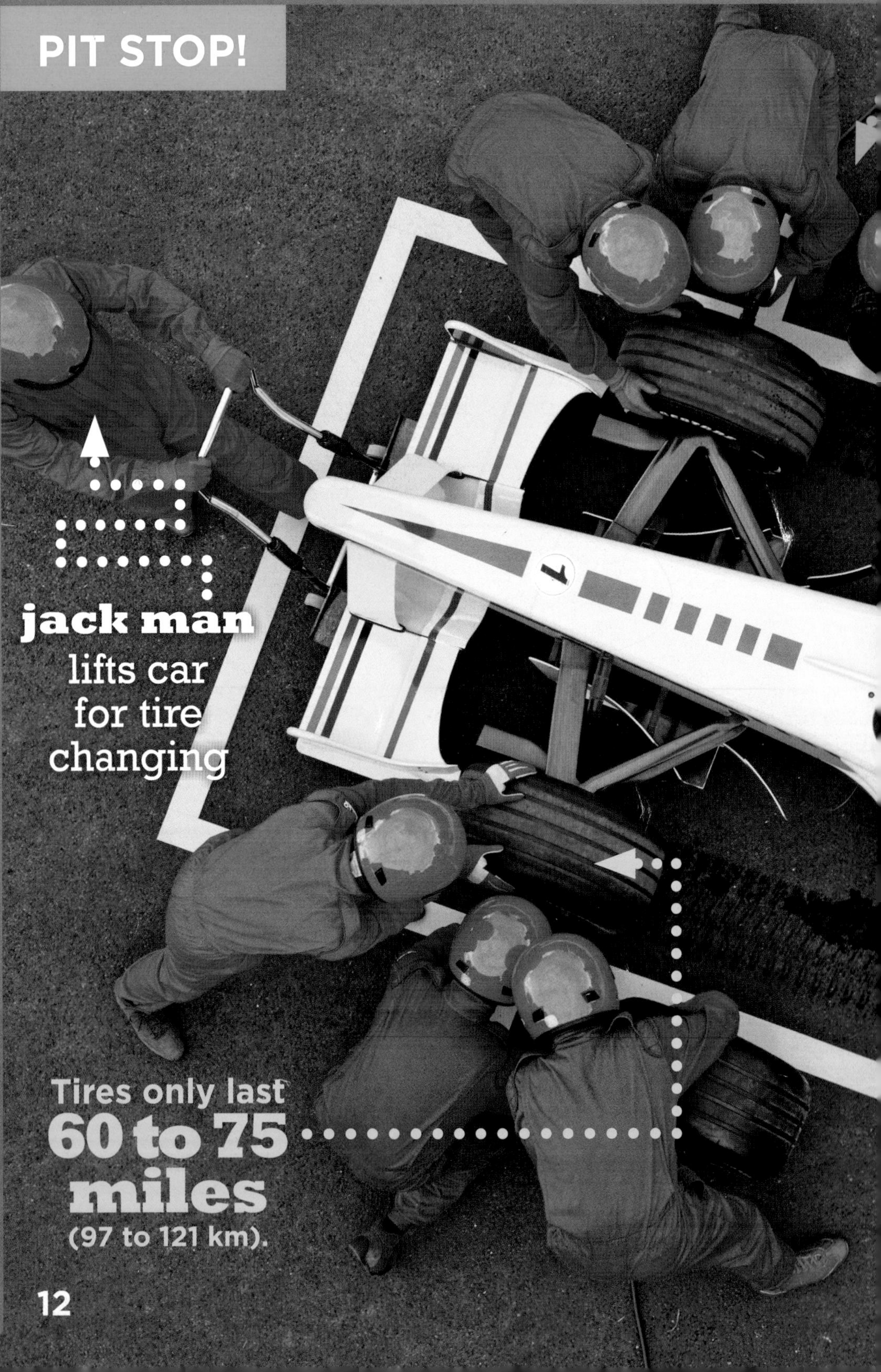

jack man
lifts car
for tire
changing

Tires only last
**60 to 75
miles**
(97 to 121 km).

Pit crews take **3 seconds** to refuel and change tires.

Crews use **air guns** to screw off and on the wheel nuts.

13

Danger Lurks

F1 racing started in 1950.
It has always been a dangerous sport.
Many drivers have died. Today's
F1 cars have many safety features.
Drivers must wear **HANS devices**
to protect their heads.

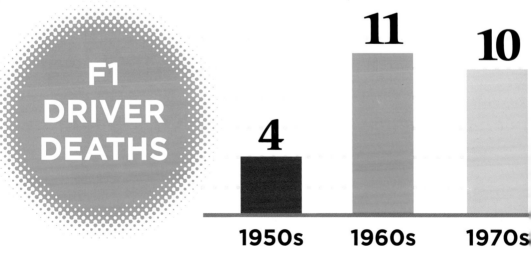

2 1980s

2 1990s

0 2000s

1 2010s

(THROUGH 2015)

CHAPTER 3

High-Tech and High Speed

F1 cars are built for speed. They have single seats and no roofs. The engines sit behind the drivers.

F1 racing has rules about car designs. That is why all the cars look alike. Teams make many little changes to go faster.

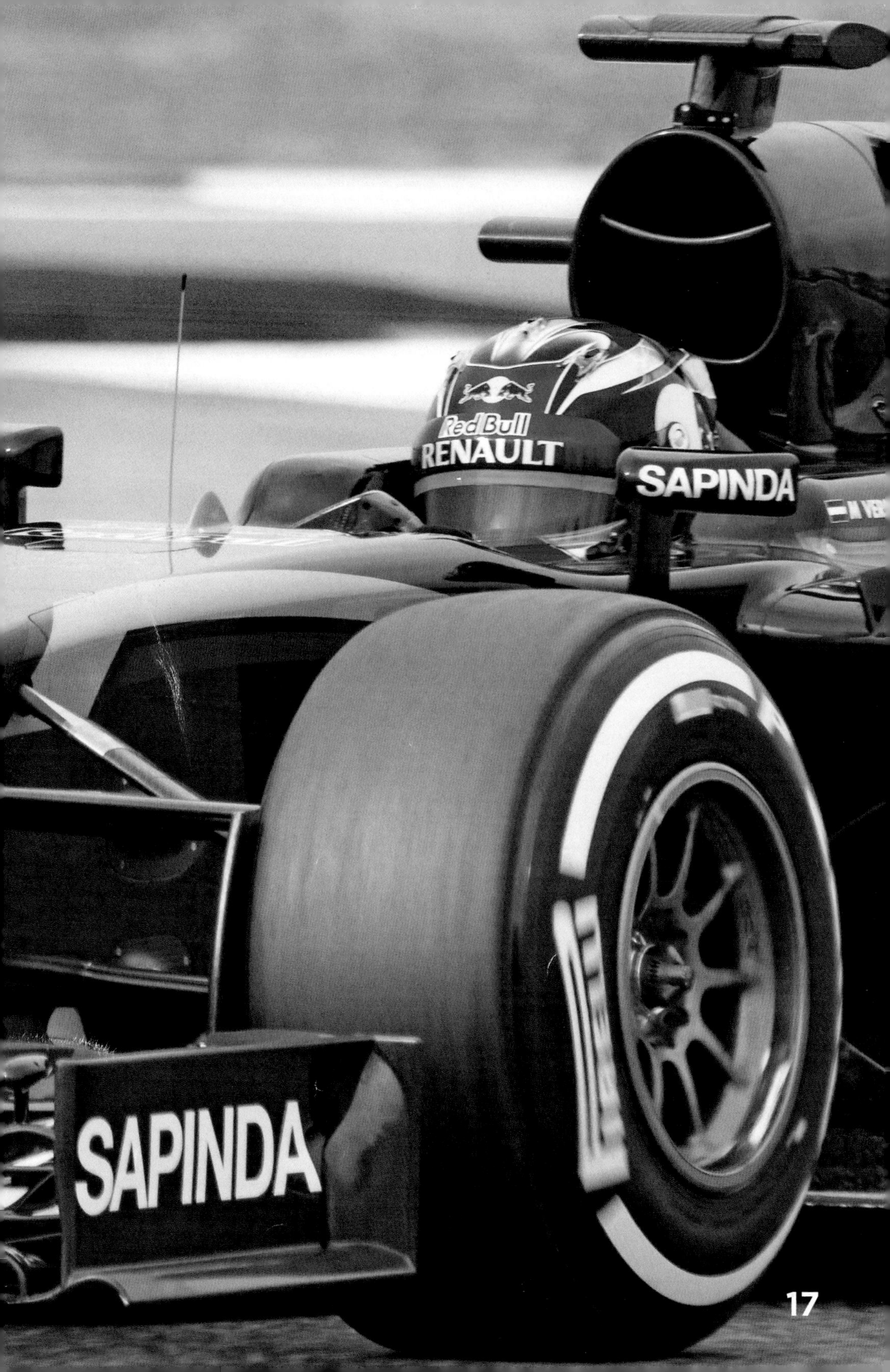
Red Bull
RENAULT
SAPINDA
SAPINDA

PARTS OF AN F1 CAR

REAR WING

SIDEPOD

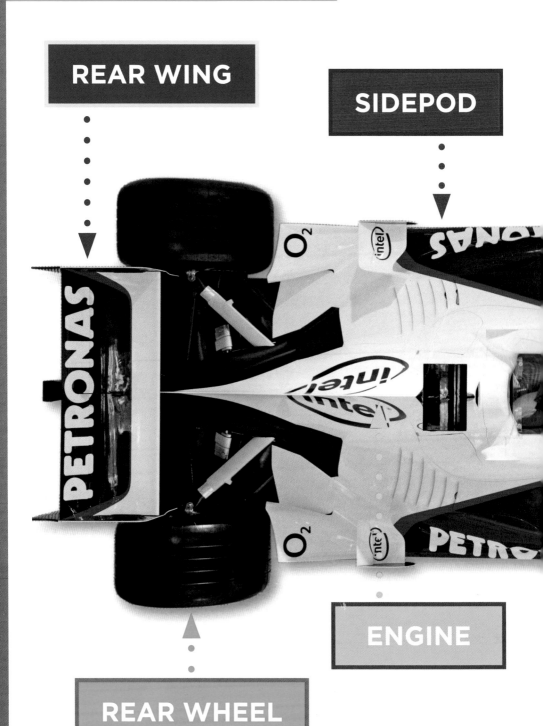

ENGINE

REAR WHEEL

FRONT WHEEL

STEERING WHEEL

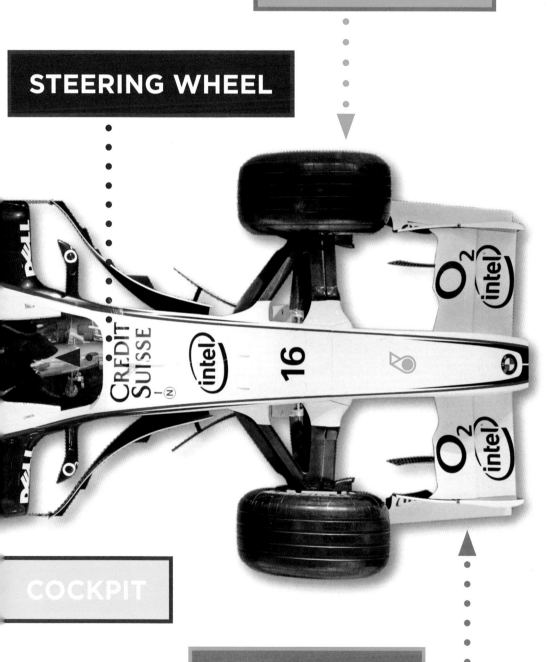

COCKPIT

FRONT WING

19

More Power!

The team with the strongest engine wins. Today's cars use 1.6-liter V-6 engines. They also use **turbos** to boost power.

F1 cars need **grip** to go fast around corners. Big wings use air to push down on the car. Wide, sticky tires give even more grip.

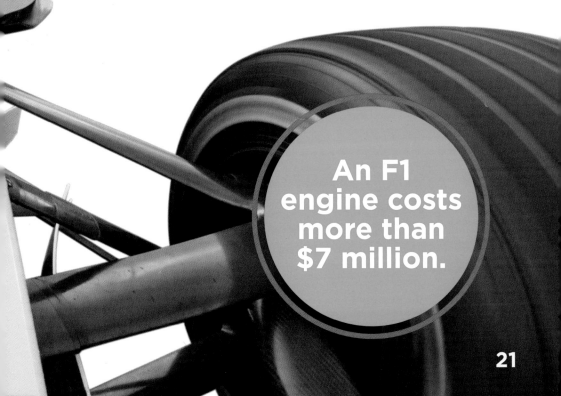

An F1 engine costs more than $7 million.

CHAPTER 4

The Future of F1

F1 racing began in Europe. Today, F1 cars race all around the world. Fans want to see faster, more exciting races. Teams are always trying to improve their cars.

COMPARING SPEEDS
AT THE MONACO F1 RACE

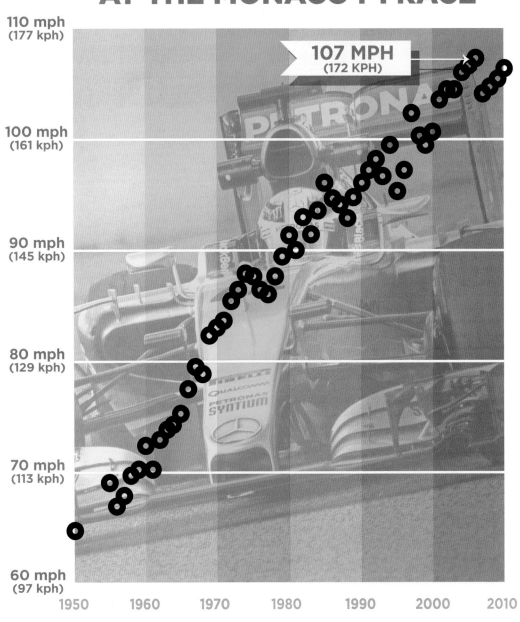

POLE POSITION SPEED

110 mph
(177 kph)

100 mph
(161 kph)

90 mph
(145 kph)

80 mph
(129 kph)

70 mph
(113 kph)

60 mph
(97 kph)

107 MPH
(172 KPH)

1950　1960　1970　1980　1990　2000　2010

MONACO F1 GRAND PRIX

FAMOUS F1 RACETRACKS

SILVERSTONE IN ENGLAND

MONTE CARLO IN MONACO

INTERLAGOS IN BRAZIL

SPA-FRANCORCHAMPS
IN BELGIUM

SUZUKA
IN JAPAN

ÖSTERREICHRING
IN AUSTRIA

ISTANBUL PARK
IN TURKEY

IMOLA IN ITALY

MARINA BAY
STREET CIRCUIT
IN SINGAPORE

MELBOURNE GRAND PRIX
CIRCUIT IN AUSTRALIA

Gas + Electric

F1 teams often use new technology. F1 cars can now capture energy from their moving parts. That energy is changed to electricity. The electricity then gives the cars a power boost.

F1 teams have always pushed the limits of speed. No one knows what F1 cars will look like in the future.

1950

First modern-era F1 race.

1961

Phil Hill becomes the first American F1 world champion.

1978

Mario Andretti becomes the second American F1 world champion.

1950

The first people walk on the moon.

1969

The United States celebrates 200 years as a nation.

1976

The Mount St. Helens volcano erupts.

1980

1994

Driver Ayrton Senna dies in a crash. This crash leads to many safety changes.

2010

Sebastian Vettel of Germany becomes the youngest F1 race winner.

2016

Terrorists attack the World Trade Center and Pentagon.

2001

GLOSSARY

ad (AD)—something that sells a product; ad is short for advertisement.

billboard (bil-BORD)—a large sign for ads

grip (GRIP)—the ability to hold firmly

HANS device (HANS de-VYS)—a safety item in many car racing sports; HANS is short for head and neck support.

horsepower (HORS-pow-uhr)—a unit used to measure the power of engines

national (NAH-shun-uhl)—relating to a country

turbo (TUR-bo)—a device that helps an engine increase power; turbo is short for turbocharger.

visor (VI-zur)—a piece on the front of a helmet that protects the face

BOOKS

Challen, Paul. *Formula 1 Racing.* Checkered Flag. New York: PowerKids Press, 2015.

MacArthur, Collin. *Inside a Formula 1 Car.* Life in the Fast Lane. New York: Cavendish Square Publishing, 2015.

Mason, Paul. *Formula 1.* Motorsports. Mankato, MN: Amicus, 2011.

WEBSITES

F1 for Kidz
f1forkidz.com/

Formula 1
www.formula1.com/

Formula 1 Games
www.kibagames.com/Formula-1-Games

INDEX